CHEYENNE the CAT
Book 2: NO GIRLS ALLOWED!

Written By:
Amanda Eaddy Oliver
Illustrated By: Brian Bear

ISBN: **0615850006**
ISBN 13: **9780615850009**

I dedicate this book to my daughter, Aaliyah. My real life, adventurous, strong- willed and determined baby girl. You can be anything that you want in life! No matter what! Shoot for the stars. I love you!

Mommy

~ Chapter One ~

~ Chapter One ~
"Just a Bad Dream"

"Mama, Mama, help" was all Roxy needed to hear before jumping out of her bed and running to her daughter's room. There she found Cheyenne, a charcoal black, sunset orange and powdered sugar white kitten quivering with the covers over her head.

"What is wrong, my dear kitten?" Roxy had never seen her child ever terrified of anything. Even during lighting storms and with the walls of their tiny cottage rattling, Cheyenne would laugh and prance around the house.

"It's daddy, Mama. Something happened to daddy!" the kitten shouted. Cheyenne loved her father so much that she could feel when something was wrong. Her little frame shook as she explained her dream to her concerned mother.

In Cheyenne's dream, Raul, the heroic general in the Feline Army, had been captured by the leader of the Birdhouse Raiders. The Birdhouse Raiders were cats that loved to eat birds. They were enemies of the Feline Army. While the cats in the Feline Army were fighting for the freedom of birds, the cats in the Birdhouse Raiders were capturing and torturing any birds that they could find. This started the Pigeon War.

"Zeke has him, Mama. Daddy needs our help." Cheyenne cried. Roxy, being the overprotective and cautious mother she was, scooped her little kitten in her arms. Roxy knew that sometimes Cheyenne could make up some silly stories. Some so convincing that Roxy would almost believe them, but this was one story she refused to think was real.

"It was just a bad dream, sweetheart." Roxy said unconvincingly. Raul had sent letters home about the Birdhouse Raiders and how rambunctious and dangerous those cats were. Especially their evil leader, Zeke.

According to Raul, Zeke used to be a part of the Feline Army. "He wasn't always this way" Raul wrote. Zeke joined the Feline Army determined and eager to help ensure all birds were free. He worked harder than any of the other cats that first joined. He dedicated his time and energy to being the best. Unfortunately, he became arrogant and wanted to be in charge, working against Raul instead of with him. When Raul became a general, Zeke couldn't handle it. He started to change. He would sneak out of camp in the middle of the night never returning until late the next day. Zeke was absent from meetings, and sometimes had what appeared to be feathers on his clothes. In time, it was revealed that Zeke was eating birds and secretly joining other cats that ate them too. When ordered to give up the distasteful passion, Zeke refused and was kicked out of the Feline Army. Before fleeing, Zeke informed Raul with a laugh and a sneer that he would see him again. Soon, the Birdhouse Raiders with Zeke as their leader, attacked birdhouses, woods, and forests everywhere in search for birds to eat.

Roxy shivered at the thought of Raul being taken by someone so cruel. Though her heart pumped faster than normal and sweat started to wet her furry paws, she continued to comfort Cheyenne.

Cheyenne knew her mother didn't want to believe her dream was true. As she rested in her warm arms, listening to Roxy's heart pound, she began to brainstorm a plan to save her father. Maybe Sebastian would be willing to help. He was her only friend in the woods and knew how much she loved her father. She could only hope that he wouldn't get all ''frightened" on her and decide to stay home. She would need him. But first things first: she had to get away from mama because she knew this wasn't "just a bad dream".

～ Chapter Two ～
-A Symphony "Less" Golden-

Getting away from mama was definitely a struggle for Cheyenne. Roxy knew her kitten was up to something. She tried to keep her in the house as long as she could. Unfortunately, she began to run out of reasons. It was a beautiful day outside and Roxy knew Sebastian and Cheyenne missed playing together. So, she reluctantly allowed Cheyenne to leave her eyesight for awhile so she could figure out how to get in contact with Raul.

Cheyenne excitedly went to look for Sebastian. She had a feeling on where to find him. The dark chocolate brown pug absolutely loved the Golden Symphony. Cheyenne laughed when she thought about their first encounter by the beautiful pond. Sebastian had been in awe of the goldfish singing in the pond and had fallen in when he tried to touch one of their heads. She was excited to see her only friend. Even though they both were different, they got along very well. Sebastian with his "smile frown" as she jokingly called it fit well with her adventurous nature.

As Cheyenne continued to remember their good times, she soon came upon her chocolate friend sitting next to the sparkling pond. Since Sebastian had his back to her, she was able to sneak behind him for a scare.

"Arrrrghhhhh!" she screamed.

Sebastian was so frightened that he fell into the Golden Symphony's waters which caused the goldfish to shriek in surprise. Cheyenne couldn't help herself and began to laugh uncontrollably. The pug wasn't amused. He didn't understand why his best friend enjoyed her pranks so much. He had to admit that her mischievousness wasn't as bad lately. While she helped him regain confidence in himself, he did his best to encourage her to be less impulsive and to "stop and think". He truly enjoyed their friendship, but would love for her to be able to make friends with the other animals in the woods. Yet, they were a perfect team. Unfortunately, their strong bond could change once Cheyenne found out what he had done.

The soggy pug crawled out of the pond with a smile on his chocolate face. Everyone in the woods knew that when Sebastian smiled he was upset about something. Since he had Cheyenne in his life, he seemed to frown more than ever. His mother and siblings didn't understand why he cared so much about the kitten.

"She is nothing but trouble, Sebastian. None of the other animals' mothers will allow her to play with them." his mother would exclaim.

He didn't care what anybody else had to say. He owed Cheyenne his life. Who knew what would have happened if his "dogmother" hadn't been there to rescue him from those ferocious pits? He began to shudder not only because of his wet fur but at the thought of how his secret would affect their friendship.

"What's wrong, Sebastian?" Cheyenne questioned. Before he could answer, Cheyenne quickly apologized for scaring him into the pond again.

"I know it was wrong, but you have to get over it fast. We have a major crisis! It's about my daddy!" the kitten cried.

Sebastian tried to listen carefully to her ramble on about her father being taken by Zeke, the leader of the Birdhouse Raiders in her dream. Even though her mother didn't believe her dream to be true, she knew it was. They had to come up with a plan. They would run way, rescue her father and save the day.

"Just like I did when I was your "dogmother", Sebastian! Sebastain? SEBASTIAN, are you listening to me?" Cheyenne shouted. Now wasn't the time to be ignored. She needed her daddy back. Safe and unharmed! She missed his hyena laugh. She longed to smell the fragrance of a medium well steak sizzling in the kitchen. She looked forward to their laying next to the pond while enjoying the majestic sounds of the Golden Symphony. Didn't Sebastian understand that? Maybe he didn't believe her either.

As she sat down on the rock beside the pond, she didn't notice her small friend reaching out to stop her. She didn't pay any attention to the widening of his smile. All she needed to hear were her goldfish singing. They always knew how to make her feel better. Putting her paw in the water, she gave them the signal to begin their sweet symphony. Unfortunately, no music came forth. And no music meant a grumpy Cheyenne.

Cheyenne stared at the goldfish in the pond wondering what would cause them not to sing on signal. What she saw was just as bad as the possibility of Raul being taken by the Birdhouse Raiders. One of the goldfish was missing! Of course they couldn't sing! There were five goldfish in the Golden Symphony. Not four! Cheyenne couldn't believe this was happening. What else could go wrong?

Sebastian watched the tears flow down the saddened kitten's face. He wished she would say something but she never said a word. He knew he should be honest and explain why a fish was missing. But his lack of confidence wouldn't let him. So, instead he sat beside his friend as she looked at the weary faces of a "Symphony Less Golden".

Chapter Three

Nothing "Nice" about "Sugar and Spice"

Even though Cheyenne was upset about a fish missing from the Golden Symphony, she knew she couldn't let that stop her! She was on a mission to rescue her daddy. That was more important than anything else in the world. This eased Sebastian's nerves and gave him time to come up with a plan to be honest and to return the goldfish. Not telling the truth was causing Sebastian too much heartache.

Cheyenne absolutely loved adventures and searching for her daddy would be the best adventure yet! She knew that setting out on this journey would be too risky alone. She desperately needed the assistance of the little pug.

"Sebastian, please say that you will go with me?" pleaded the kitten.

Sebastian smiled at her revealing his displeasure in her request.

"Cheyenne, I don't know about this. How do you know that your dream is true? Plus, we don't know where to find him!" he exclaimed.

"Just trust me, pug." Cheyenne jokingly said. She had to find a way to convince Sebastian, her mother Roxy, as well as herself that this was the right thing to do.

"How are we going to get away from our moms?" Sebastian whined. His mother already thought that Cheyenne was trouble. He didn't believe that she would let him go anywhere with the kitten. Cheyenne thought about that too. After a while of deep thinking, she came up with the only plan that she felt would work.

"We just won't tell them." She exclaimed.

"Whaaatttt? Are you crazy?!" the little pug shouted. Not telling his mother about his whereabouts wouldn't work. That would be another secret. His little body couldn't handle anymore secrets. Cheyenne could see that convincing Sebastian to join her on her adventure was taking a lot of work.

"Okay, we will write them a letter telling them of our plans. Once they have the letter, maybe they won't be as worried." she hoped. Cheyenne knew that her mother worried about a lot. She also knew that she was the major cause of her mother's worries. There were times when she wished she could be all that her mother hoped her to be. Calm, quiet, lover of peanut butter and jelly sandwiches, and all of that other "girly stuff". But Cheyenne wasn't that girl. She was inquisitive, adventurous and strong-willed. She was determined to be a general in the Feline Army just like her daddy. She wasn't going to allow anyone or anything to keep her from accomplishing that goal. Rescuing her father would prove to everyone that she had what it took to get the job done. Even if he didn't need rescuing!

Sebastian cared so much about his best friend and knew he couldn't allow her to go on this journey alone. He had to trust her plan and believe that his mother wouldn't be TOO mad when she found out. Who knows? This adventure may be fun.

"Okay, cat, I'll go with you." Sebastian jokingly said.

"Yippee!" Cheyenne hollered with great joy!

Let the adventure begin!

That evening the two friends hurriedly worked on the letter they would leave for their mothers.

Dear Momma:

Please don't be worried! I just want to find my daddy! I know you don't believe in my dream but I do! I could be wrong but I won't rest until I find out that he is safe. Please don't be mad! As soon as I find out that he is safe, I will head straight home! I promise! You are the best momma that a cat could ever have. I love you.
Cheyenne

Cheyenne knew that this letter would cause uproar in her mother. There was a strong possibility that she would come after her. Even if that happened, Cheyenne hoped that they would be too far along for her to catch them.

Sebastian watched as Cheyenne wrote her letter. He hadn't the slightest idea of what to say to his mother. When Cheyenne handed him the pen, he wrote the first thing that came to his mind.

Dear Mommy,
I'm with the cat!
Sebastian

Cheyenne looked at what Sebastian had written and shook her head. All the worried pug could do was to shrug his shoulders. Deep inside, he hoped that this new adventure wouldn't end in a disaster.

Roxy had a feeling that her kitten was up to something when she went to bed without a fuss. Usually, Cheyenne had one hundred and one reasons for it not being bedtime. Not that night! Cheyenne allowed Roxy to tuck her in and even gave her mother an extra long kiss on the cheek.

"That was just too easy." Roxy thought. The mother's over protective nature wouldn't allow her to sleep just yet. Roxy still anxiously waited for a letter from the general yet none arrived. Instead of worrying, she sat in the little armchair near their cottage door and read some of his old letters. After drinking a few caramel lattes, Roxy drifted off to sleep.

Cheyenne peeked out of her room and saw her mother sleeping in the armchair by the front door. "Drat!" she whispered. If she couldn't go out of the front door, she guessed she would have to move on to plan B. The chimney! After leaving her letter on the table, the adventurous kitten tiptoed past her mother and began the tedious journey up the chimney walls.

As she climbed, she begged herself "Please don't sneeze, please don't sneeze" for she knew that her sneezing would send her back down the chimney and would wake her mother up for sure. Finally, she made it to the top and out of the chimney, gasping and gagging while trying to dust the black soot off her body. When she realized that it was going to take more time than she had to get herself clean, she gave up.

"No problem" she said. "The soot can be my camouflage!" The kitten laughed, scurrying down the house to the Golden Symphony where she was to meet Sebastian.

Sebastian was a nervous wreck when Cheyenne arrived that he didn't notice how dirty her appearance was. He too had waited until his mother was asleep before he made the great escape of his life.

"Are you sure you want to do this, Cheyenne" he asked. Sebastian was torn between disappointing his mother and his best friend. But he felt obligated to his best friend. Especially when he was hiding such a huge secret from her.

"Of course I am sure, Sebastian!" Cheyenne replied. The kitten was becoming frustrated with the pug and everyone else who didn't understand her. She wasn't the typical female kitten that loved having tea parties. She wasn't easily understood by the animals in the woods. She was Cheyenne, the kitten with a mind of her own and her mind was set on finding her daddy. She wasn't a scaredy-cat! And there was absolutely nothing " nice" about sugar and spice.

"Sebastian, it will be ok. Trust me! Just think of it like this. It will be the first time ever that I owe you something"!

After hearing those words from his friend, Sebastian knew that she wouldn't be taking this journey alone. His smile frown returned as he became excited about the adventures ahead of them.

Cheyenne jumped with glee as she saw the frown form on the pug's face. That's when the soot on her fur was noticed.

"What happened to you?" the pug asked.

"What? You don't like it? It's part of my uniform. Its camouflage!" the kitten laughed.

With a shake of his head, Sebastian helped his adventurous friend clean the soot off her clothes. Soon after, they began the rescue of their lives.

Chapter Four
The "Ouchy" Truth

Roxy woke up with a start and knew that her kitten was gone.

"Cheyenne!" she screamed. When she didn't receive an answer she walked to her kitten's room and saw an empty bed. Roxy couldn't believe that Cheyenne would leave without saying anything. Didn't she know that her mother would be worried?

Walking back to the little armchair, Roxy spotted a slip of paper on the table and knew that it was from Cheyenne. After reading her kitten's note, she decided to write a letter of her own. She hoped that it would be received in the nick of time.

Cheyenne hadn't a clue where she was going. Her daddy had told her that towards the end of the Pigeon War, the Feline Army would be camped out close to home. She could picture the troops scattered across the land at different campfires discussing the day's events. Though there were over a hundred campfires, all of the smoke came together and made one gigantic black cloud. Her daddy stated it was the sign of the Feline Army's unity. Cheyenne was tired, but she allowed the remembrance of her father's heartbeat to push her forward.

Unfortunately, Sebastian couldn't keep his eyes open any longer.

"Cheyenne, can we please take a break?" the pug whined. Cheyenne knew Sebastian needed his sleep if he was going to be any good for the remainder of their journey. After traveling a little longer, the friends spotted a tiny cave. Cheyenne decided that the cave would be their resting place for the night. As soon as the little pug entered the cave, he found a corner and got comfortable. He was fast asleep before Cheyenne could utter "good night". It took awhile but Cheyenne found her own little corner and allowed the soft sounds of the pug's snores to put her to sleep.

Raul held the letter from his dear Roxy in his hand. It had arrived that morning and the details were shocking. He didn't know what else he expected from his inquisitive kitten. So, she thought he had been captured by Zeke because of a dream, huh? He had to shake his head and laugh. When he found her, they would definitely have to discuss which dreams she could run away with.

Zeke may be a little threatening to the other soldiers, but to Raul, he was harmless. After this last battle, Raul was confident that Zeke wouldn't show his face for a very long time. As Raul stared at his troops lounging around the campfires, sharing stories and laughing, his heart began to sink. The one thing he wasn't confident about was whether his kitten would ever heal after hearing the "ugly truth". He knew she would find him. He had taught her well. She possessed all the qualities needed to be a great general one day. Unfortunately, that day would never arrive. As much as he told Cheyenne that she could be anything that she wanted, he never imagined how serious she would be about following in his footsteps. Their relationship was special and he hoped that it stayed that way. How Cheyenne would react to finding out that no girls were allowed in the Feline Army worried him.

Raul glanced over Roxy's letter one more time, looked into the sky, and said a little prayer for the safety of his kitten and her friend. If she remembered what he had told her about the unity cloud of smoke, she would find him in no time. All there was left to do was to sit and wait.

Sebastian woke up to the sun shining into the dark cave. Surprisingly, Cheyenne was still fast asleep. As he watched his friend snore, he knew that he had to tell her the truth. The longer he kept it from her, the harder it got for him inside. He didn't know how she would handle hearing that her best friend stole a goldfish from her. He didn't do it to be mean or nasty. When Sebastian was not with Cheyenne, he was lonely. Having one of the goldfish was like having a piece of her when they were a part. Once he brought the goldfish home, it refused to sing. A fish bowl could never compare to being able to swim freely in the majestic waters of the pond. Sebastian knew that he had to return the fish back to the Golden Symphony as soon as he got home.

At that moment, Cheyenne sat up and stared at the chocolate pug. She noticed his smile and knew something was wrong. But before she could ask, Sebastian spoke.

"I took the fish!" he exclaimed.

At first, Cheyenne was confused, but then a light bulb went off in her head. When she needed the goldfish to sing for her, they wouldn't because a fish was missing. That day she needed to hear their music. It made her feel like she was closer to her daddy. To think that her best friend was the reason why she wasn't able to have that experience brought her to tears.

"You took my fish? Why would you do that, Sebastian?" Cheyenne cried.

Sebastian disliked seeing his friend in this state. He tried to console her the best way he knew how.

"I didn't mean to hurt you. You see, when I am at home, I have no one to talk to. You have no idea how much our friendship means to me, Cheyenne. You are my only friend. I thought if I had the fish, it would make me less lonely because I had a part of you. I am so sorry, Cheyenne. As soon as we get home, I promise to put it back. Please forgive me!" the pug begged.

Cheyenne recalled how her mother stressed the importance of never holding grudges and always giving someone another chance. Roxy stated that one day, Cheyenne would need a second chance. Sebastian was a great friend. The fact that he agreed to come on this trip proved his loyalty. He had made a big mistake, but he deserved her forgiveness.

"Yes, I will forgive you, Sebastian. For now on, will you please ask before taking something of mine?" Cheyenne asked.

The little pug squealed for joy and promised his friend that he would never take anything else that didn't belong to him without asking.

"No more time for standing around, pug." the kitten exclaimed. "Let's get this show on the road."

The two friends restarted the long journey of finding Cheyenne's father. After seeming like they had traveled for miles, Sebastian spotted the most beautiful sight he had ever seen in the sky. As Cheyenne turned to look at the thing that had the pug amazed, tears came to her eyes. There was the gigantic black cloud of smoke. They had made it! The kitten's heart began to beat super fast as she thought of how close she was to rescuing her father. Little her had traveled without her parents and nothing bad happened.

Raul looked up and saw his kitten as she entered the campsite. She was still the spitting image of her mother. With so much love in his heart, he jumped up and ran towards his child. Cheyenne shrieked as she saw her daddy running towards her unharmed.

"Daddy, Daddy!" she cried. "You're safe. Oh I am so glad that you are safe."

Raul swung Cheyenne around and around until they became dizzy. Raul fell on the ground with his daughter in his arms, both of them laughing joyfully.

"I missed you so much, Daddy."Cheyenne said. "I had a bad dream that Zeke had captured you."

"I missed you too, sweetheart. I am sorry that you had such a bad dream about me. But I want you to know that if anything were to happen to me, it wouldn't be because of Zeke's doing. He's not as strong as your dad!" Raul, Cheyenne, and Sebastian looked at each other and then began to laugh hysterically.

"That's right, because I have the strongest daddy in the world!" Cheyenne shouted. With that, Raul scooped Cheyenne up on his shoulders and took Sebastian's hand.

"It is time to get you two home." the general exclaimed. Cheyenne and Sebastian couldn't agree with him more. They both missed their mothers. After having to sleep on a hard ground, they missed their beds too.

"Hopefully Momma won't be too mad at me, right, Daddy?" Cheyenne asked.

"I don't know if I can save you from this one, kiddo." Raul admitted. "But I will see what I can do."Cheyenne smiled as she thought about how her daddy always saved the day. She was so much like him in more ways than one. After today's attempted rescue, she knew that being a general was in her near future. She hoped that her daddy felt the same way.

~ Chapter Five ~
A First Time for Everything

Raul made sure that Cheyenne and Sebastian made it safely back to the woods. He returned Sebastian home to a frantic mother. Raul listened as she scolded Sebastian and stated how she didn't want him playing with Cheyenne anymore. After being coaxed by the general and the two friends promising never to pull a stunt like they had ever again, the pug's mother agreed to give their friendship another chance. Raul felt that deep down inside she knew that the two were inseparable. Keeping them a part would do more damage than good.

It was as if Roxy knew that her two loves had returned. She met them at the door. Her heart beamed at the sight of Raul in his general uniform. She knew that after writing the letter, he would find and bring their only child back to her. Before chastising her, Roxy wrapped her warm arms around her kitten's body, taking in her scent. The fact that she needed a bath didn't even bother her, but she knew that receiving one later would be enough punishment for the kitten.

"I'm sorry I had you worried, Momma. You were right about my dream." Cheyenne admitted.

"It is okay, my love. I am just so happy that you two are home safe." Roxy exclaimed as she continued to squeeze and kiss Cheyenne until she had enough.

"It was a great adventure, but I am so tired." The kitten stretched and yawned. She hoped her mother would let her go to bed without a bath just this once. Unfortunately, that didn't happen.

After receiving an unwanted tongue bath and scolding from her mother, Cheyenne was given permission to go to bed. Raul was waiting for her at her bedside with a purple box. Once Cheyenne was comfortably tucked in, Raul decided to break the news to his kitten.

"You did a brave thing today, my sweet. And I am very proud of you." the general stated.

Cheyenne beamed and attentively listened to what her daddy was saying. She didn't want to miss any information that could help her be better prepared for becoming a general. Sadly, the next words that Raul spoke brought tears to her eyes.

"Cheyenne, I know how much you want to be a general in the Feline Army. It has always been a dream of yours. I am sorry to say that your dream will never happen, honey, because no girls are allowed to join." Raul said.

He watched as his daughter stared in disbelief. His heart broke as the tears fell from the hazelnuts in her eyes. He felt responsible for allowing this dream to get out of hand. Cheyenne's determination to become something she could never be could have gotten her hurt.

"I know you don't understand, my love. I have always told you that you could be anything you ever wanted. Oh, how I wish that were true." Raul continued.

Cheyenne refused to speak. Maybe if she was quiet, she would wake up from this horrible nightmare.

Raul hoped that giving Cheyenne what was in the purple box would eventually mend her broken heart. He opened the box to reveal a gold medal. Raul had received the medal when he first became a general. It was a medal of honor and meant a lot to him. It could never mean as much to him as Cheyenne.

"Sweetie, I want you to have this Medal of Honor. It was given to me once I became a general in the Feline Army. I know it can't replace your dream of becoming one, but every time you look at it, I want you to remember that you will always be a "general" to me." Raul placed the medal in Cheyenne's white paws, kissed her on her furry head, and left her bedroom.

The kitten stared at her daddy's medal while taking in everything he had said. No girls allowed in the Feline Army? That couldn't be true. She tried to remember if she had seen any females at the campsite. No, she had not! Honestly, she had never seen her daddy talk about his female soldiers. As she thought about the reasons why girls weren't allowed, a thought popped into her head.

"Maybe the reason why girls aren't allowed is because there hasn't been a girl who has ever wanted to join." the kitten wondered out loud. "Maybe I am supposed to be the first!" she exclaimed to herself.

Soon Cheyenne's sadness started to fade and was replaced with hope. She knew that becoming a general in the Feline Army was a part of her destiny and refused to give up on her dream that easily. Her determination wouldn't let her.

"I will show everyone." she whispered as she kissed her daddy's Medal of Honor. One day, she too would have a medal of her own. There's always a first time for everything!